BILLY SURE

·KID ENTREPRENEUR·

AND THE INVISIBLE INVENTOR

INVENTED BY **LUKE SHARPE**
DRAWINGS BY **GRAHAM ROSS**

Simon Spotlight

New York   London   Toronto   Sydney   New Delhi

SIMON SPOTLIGHT

An imprint of Simon & Schuster Children's Publishing Division

1230 Avenue of the Americas, New York, New York 10020

This Simon Spotlight hardcover edition July 2016

Copyright © 2016 by Simon & Schuster, Inc. Text by Michael Teitelbaum.

Illustrations by Graham Ross. All rights reserved, including the right of reproduction in whole or in part in any form.

SIMON SPOTLIGHT and colophon are registered trademarks of Simon & Schuster, Inc.

For information about special discounts for bulk purchases, please contact Simon & Schuster Special Sales at 1-866-506-1949 or business@simonandschuster.com.

Designed by Jay Colvin

The text of this book was set in Minya Nouvelle.

Manufactured in the United States of America 0616 FFG

10 9 8 7 6 5 4 3 2 1

ISBN 978-1-4814-6197-9 (hc)

ISBN 978-1-4814-6196-2 (pbk)

ISBN 978-1-4814-6198-6 (eBook)

Library of Congress Catalog Card Number 2015958256

Chapter One

One Big Happy Family

USUALLY DINNERTIME AT MY HOUSE ISN'T SOMETHING to look forward to. My dad likes to make all kinds of wacky dishes. My mom travels a lot for work, so she's often not around. And my sister, Emily . . . let's just say she's not the nicest person in the world, all the time.

But tonight, dinner is different. That's because my family—and my best friend—are gathered around the kitchen table, eating the best take-out pizza in the whole wide world!

For those of you who may not have heard of me, my name is Billy Sure. I am one half of

SURE THINGS, INC., an invention company that I share with my best friend—and current pizza-eating pal—Manny Reyes.

About a week ago Manny, my dad, Emily, and I returned from an unplanned adventure at the Really Great Movies studio. Manny, Emily, and I got to play zombies in a new movie, *Alien Zombie Attack!* It's funny to think about it, because this all started when Emily stole my latest invention, a hovercraft, and crash-landed at the studio. We had to rescue her.

While at the movie studio, we sold the hovercraft—renamed the REALLY GREAT HOVERCRAFT—to the film's director, so he can use it in his movies.

But Manny, being the super businessman that he is, kept all the hovercraft's merchandising rights for Sure Things, Inc. That means profit from any products related to the hovercraft gets to stay ours. Pretty smart, huh? Because he sweats the fine print of every business deal is reason #934 why I'm glad that Manny is my best friend and business partner.

Although this happened a week ago, it still feels like just yesterday. On the actual "just yesterday," my mom came back from her latest work trip. I say "work trip," but it's much cooler than that—my mom is a spy. She's away on different missions a lot.

For her current mission Mom is able to work remotely from home. I really miss her when she's not around, so it's great having her here, for lots of reasons. One of those reasons is that, unlike my dad, Mom loves to order in food—like this super-awesome TWELVE-CHEESE PIZZA!

"I didn't even know there were twelve different kinds of cheeses," Mom says, biting into her slice.

Dad munches happily, pausing every so often to smile and say "yum!" These days, Dad seems to have a permanent smile on his face. And for good reason.

"I can't believe my art show is just a few days away," Dad says through a mouthful of cheese. "But I wonder if I need another painting of Philo's paw for the show. . . ."

Oh yeah, I forgot to tell you. Dad may be a terrible cook, but he's a terrific artist. I *think*. I guess I don't know much about art. His latest series of paintings is going to be displayed at a gallery. They are mostly paintings of my dog Philo's tongue, Philo's paws, and oddly enough, Philo's butt.

Dad also has a few paintings of some of the food he's made, like tomato pancakes and cherry and kiwi lasagna. The paintings may just be tastier than the food itself—though I've never taken a bite out of one.

I've finished my first slice of pizza when I hear Manny's voice.

"Ready for another one?" he asks from across the table.

"Thanks, partner, but I can get it myself," I reply. "You don't have to get up."

"Who said anything about getting up?"

Manny pulls out his smartphone and taps the screen. From across the room, a slice of pizza comes flying through the air, right at me!

4

"Manny!" I cry. "Did you invent **FLYING PIZZA?!**"

Before Manny can answer, I snatch the slice out of the air. There, hanging in the air, is a small, perfectly accurate model of the Really Great Hovercraft! The pizza had been resting on the model.

"I didn't invent flying pizza, but I did come up with a remote controlled model of the hovercraft," Manny explains. "I control it right from my smartphone."

Manny swipes his phone, and the tiny hover-craft turns around and speeds back to the pizza boxes on the counter.

"Awesome," I say. "I think this toy is going to be a huge hit!"

"I'd like some flying pizza too," says Mom.

"Sure," Manny says.

With Manny tapping and swiping his phone, the tiny hovercraft slides under another slice, turns around, speeds back through the air, and deposits a slice of pizza onto Mom's plate.

BAM! That's when the front door bursts open. You might have noticed that my sister Emily has been absent from dinner so far. (Okay, I kind of forgot too.) That's because she was walking Philo, who scurries in, pulling hard on his leash.

"Easy, Philo!" Emily says. "Slow down!"

Are you surprised that Emily is the one walking Philo, and not me? Well, you should be. Before we returned from our trip to the Really Great Movies studio, I could count on two hands the number of times that Emily had volunteered to walk Philo.

Uh, now that I think about it . . . make that *one* hand.

But as punishment for stealing my hovercraft, Dad grounded Emily FOR LIFE. He was probably exaggerating about the lifelong sentence part, though, because he made a deal with her. If Emily is as nice and helpful as she possibly can be, and does one nice big thing for each member of our family, she will be ungrounded.

Well, since making that deal, it's like Emily is a whole new person. She takes out the garbage, cleans the dinner dishes, and volunteers to walk Philo every evening! I've been calling her SUPER NICE EMILY. I know she hates the nickname, but she has to be nice and can't say anything about it.

I could get used to this!

"I wish Philo wouldn't pull on his leash when I take him for a walk," Emily says.

Before I have a chance to explain that all she has to do is say "heel" and he'll walk nicely beside you, Philo spots the flying hovercraft toy zooming through the air.

Philo starts barking wildly at the hovercraft and takes off after it, dragging Emily through the kitchen and back into the living room. I have to admit, it's really funny. Emily jumps over a chair, then stumbles to avoid crashing into a table.

The hovercraft turns back toward the kitchen. Philo suddenly changes direction to

keep up with it, causing Emily to knock a lamp from a table.

She spins back and catches the lamp just before it hits the floor.

This is really entertaining to watch. I consider letting it go on a little longer, but, well, that would just be mean.

"Let go of the leash, Emily!" I shout, cracking up.

She lets go. Philo continues to chase the hovercraft until Manny guides it back into his hands.

Emily joins us, trying to catch her breath. Her curly hair has flopped into her face. Her shirt has come untucked. She's a mess, which normally would make her very upset and require extensive repair time in front of a mirror. But Super Nice Emily doesn't complain.

"Well, I walked Philo again," she says, forcing a smile.

"We know, dear," says Mom. "Why don't you have some pizza?"

"I will," says Emily. "But first everyone

has to come outside and see the great job I did WASHING THE CAR! And since everyone rides in the car, it's something nice I did for the *whole* family."

"You washed the car?" I ask in disbelief. Even for Super Nice Emily, this is above and beyond. "Now, *this* I have to see!"

We all get up and hurry outside.

"Well, what do you think?" asks Emily.

I look over at the car and see that it is covered in SOAP. Bubbly white streaks drip down the doors and windows.

"Maybe Dad can paint a picture of this for his art show," I say. Usually, I go out of my way not to give Emily a hard time. The grief I always get from her in return is just not worth the fun. But with her having to be nice and helpful to everybody, I figure I've got a free pass. "Dad can call the painting HALF-WASHED CAR."

"I appreciate the effort, Emily," says Mom, raising her eyebrows slightly at me. "But you have to rinse the soap off."

A few minutes later everyone except Emily is back inside, and Manny is really getting into delivering pizza slices using the hovercraft toy.

"I'll take another one, Manny," says Dad. "I'm curious how they can stuff the cheese *inside* the cheese."

Manny taps and swipes his phone, tilting it a bit left, then right. The hovercraft toy scoops up a slice of pizza, circles the living room, then comes back into the kitchen, dropping gently down until it stops, hovering in midair right above Dad's plate.

"Thanks, Manny," says Dad, taking the slice. He stares at the cheese-stuffed cheese. "Hmm . . . so *that's* how they do it."

Emily comes back inside. "Well, the car is clean," she says. "All the soap is off."

And I can see where it went. Emily's clothes are now streaked with white bubbly soapsuds! She looks wet from head to toe. I almost feel bad for her. It's probably not nice to be enjoying this as much as I am, but I am!

"You should change into some warm clothes," says Mom. "Then come have a slice of pizza."

When Emily finally sits down, Manny delivers her a slice with the mini hovercraft.

"Thank you, Manny," she says, digging into her pizza. "And congratulations on your new toy. Another Sure Things, Inc. success!"

After every slice has been devoured Emily is the first one to jump up from the table. "Here," she says. "Let me get those for everyone."

She goes around the table, picking up all the plates and cups. Then she washes, dries, and carefully puts away each one.

"There, everything's clean," she says as a glob of soapsuds (this time, from the kitchen) drops from her shirt onto her shoes.

Ding dong!

The doorbell. Hmm, we're not expecting anyone. Out of habit, I start toward the door.

"Oh, no, Billy," Emily says sweetly. "Let *me* answer the door."

I better enjoy this while I can, because I have a feeling that once Emily gets out of her grounded-for-life sentence, she's gonna make me pay for all her niceness. Big time!

Emily opens the front door.

"Hi, is Billy home?" asks a woman at the door. "I'd *love* to conduct an interview with him this evening."

I immediately feel a knot forming in my stomach. I know that voice. It's KATHY JENKINS. She's a reporter for *Right Next Door*, our local hometown news website. She's also Samantha's mother. Samantha is a member of my inventor's club, but she also helped me come up with the hovercraft design and used

13

to follow me around the halls at school.

Kathy has written articles before about Sure Things, Inc. She always focuses on me, leaving out Manny's role in the company. And she can be nasty. She even wrote one time that Philo smells like a skunk.

What could she possibly want now?

Chapter Two

The Interview

I walk over to greet Kathy.

As much as I would love to, I can't refuse to talk with the press. That wouldn't do anything good for Sure Things, Inc. And I know Manny wouldn't want that.

"How are you, Billy?" Kathy says, extending her hand.

I shake her hand. Then we both take seats in the living room.

She glances into the kitchen, where Manny is teaching Dad how to pilot the hovercraft toy. She seems unfazed.

"So," Kathy says, pressing play on her portable recorder. "Tell me about DANNY."

"Danny?" I ask. "Who's Danny?"

She raises her eyebrows as if to say, *Why are you trying to make this difficult?*

"Danny. Your partner," she repeats.

"Manny," I correct her. "His name is Manny."

I'm glad she's finally interested in Manny, but can't she get his name right?

"Yes, Manny, of course. Tell me about Manny."

Finally a chance to set the record straight.

"Well, basically, without Manny, there is no Sure Things, Inc.," I begin. "Everything we do, we do as a team. We work really well together and make every important decision as partners. The nicest part is that through it all we've been able to stay best friends. And really, I think that's why we work so well together, and why Sure Things, Inc. has been successful."

"So do you do all the inventing, and Danny handles all the business and marketing?" asks Kathy.

"Manny," I correct her. *Again.* "And for the most part that's true, but take a look at this."

I quickly download the app Manny created onto my phone. Then I tap the screen. The hovercraft toy comes flying into the living room. I swipe the screen and the toy circles the room once, then comes in for a soft landing right at my feet.

"This is the REALLY GREAT HOVERCRAFT TOY," I explain. "This was all Manny's idea. He wrote the app and built a replica of our hovercraft—only mini!"

"But I thought that Sure Things, Inc. sold the rights of the hovercraft to Really Great Movies?" says Kathy.

This is perfect. She just set me up to show how smart Manny really is.

"Well, actually, we did," I explain. "The movie studio is using the hovercraft in their movies and theme parks. But, because Manny is such a good businessperson, we kept all the merchandising rights."

I tap my phone again, and the hovercraft

toy lifts up and zooms back into the kitchen.

"I just *love* this," Kathy squeals. "Who knew that Danny was the HIDDEN FACE of Sure Things, Inc.?"

"Manny," I say, "and it's really no secret. Manny has been there from the start. He's always been a huge and equal part of the company. You know, I have tried to tell you this before. And I have tried to bring Manny in on some of our earlier interviews. But you always seem to–"

"Tell me this, Billy," Kathy interrupts me. It's clear she doesn't want to listen. "Who *really* came up with the marketing plan for the DISAPPEARING REAPPEARING MAKEUP?"

"That was Manny."

"The GROSS-TO-GOOD POWDER?"

"That was Manny too."

"Fascinating," says Kathy.

I should be happy that she's looking to give Manny credit, but I feel uneasy. I just don't trust her. Even now.

"So, it appears that Danny is extremely important to Sure Things, Inc.," Kathy says.

Why won't she use his real name?

"His name is Manny, and yes, that's what I've been trying to tell you since our very first interview."

Kathy stands up suddenly. I get up too.

"This was great, Billy," she says, shaking my hand. "Thank you for your time, and be sure to read *Right Next Door* tomorrow! We'll be happy to tell everyone about Manny."

"Danny," I hiss, and then I take it back. Oh no! Did Kathy use his correct name to trip me up?

Without saying anything, Kathy hurries to the front door and leaves just as quickly as she arrived.

I rejoin the others in the kitchen.

"I can't believe her!" I say, grabbing my head with both hands.

"What happened?" asks Mom.

I fill everyone in on the interview—including my flub at the end. Then I look right at Manny, who's been busy checking company e-mail on his phone.

"She finally wants to include your contributions and she can't even bother to get your name right!"

Manny just shakes his head and smiles.

"She can call me GRANNY for all I care," Manny says. "In fact, she can call me anything she likes, as long as she mentions Sure Things, Inc. and the Really Great Hovercraft Toy. We get publicity. We move merchandise. It's all good, Billy!"

Well, I suppose he's right, as usual.

Super Nice Emily doesn't seem to know of a way to make this situation any better, so she says, "Can I do anything for anyone else right now?" in a happy SINGSONG VOICE that I honestly have never heard her use before.

Sheesh . . . I'm starting to appreciate the old-fashioned, annoying, the-whole-world-revolves-around-Emily Emily. This new, nice version is starting to get just a *little* obnoxious.

A short while later Manny gets up to head for home.

"Thanks for the pizza," he says. "It was great."

"Well, thank *you* for the AERIAL DELIVERY!" says Dad.

"See ya tomorrow, Manny," I say.

Manny smiles. "See you tomorrow, partner. And don't worry about Kathy Jenkins. As long as Sure Things, Inc. is in the news, we're golden."

I go upstairs and finish some homework for tomorrow.

That night I toss and turn. Even though Manny said not to, I can't stop thinking about the interview. Kathy tricked me into calling Manny, Danny! I feel like the WORST BEST FRIEND.

This was supposed to be a happy, easy time for me. Mom is home. There's no pressure at the moment for me to crank out a new invention. Things are good.

And yet I have trouble sleeping.

The next day at school is actually pretty good. The interview slips further and further toward the back of my mind. Throughout the day I focus on classes and start to get excited about the upcoming release of the hovercraft toy.

As I head for the front door at the end of the school day, a voice calls out to me from behind. "Hi, Billy."

I spin around and see CLAYTON HARRIS, president of the Fillmore Middle School Inventor's Club.

"Hi, Clayton, what's up?" I ask.

"I heard about your trip to the Really Great Movies studio," says Clayton, "and all about the hovercraft. That is very cool!"

"Yeah, it was kinda wild," I say. "But it all turned out okay."

I can see Clayton being first in line to buy the hovercraft toy when it comes out.

"So, I don't know if you're planning on coming to the next inventor's club meeting, but I wanted to show you what I invented," Clayton explains.

It makes me feel good that even though he's now president of the club, Clayton still likes to show me his inventions. I did invent the inventor's club, after all. Clayton opens his backpack . . . and pulls out another backpack.

"I was inspired by your hovercraft," he says. "I call this the HOVER BACKPACK. You know how kids are always complaining about how heavy their backpacks are? Watch this."

Clayton flips a switch on the pack and it floats into the air beside him. He takes a step down the hall and the backpack follows him.

"Very cool," I say, wishing for a moment that I had thought of it.

"Now here's the part I'm still working on," Clayton says. He stops and turns toward the

hovering backpack. "SCIENCE BOOK!" he says.

A slot in the side of the pack opens and a book comes shooting out. Clayton snatches the book out of the air.

Now *that* is cool!

"Math book!" Clayton commands.

Five books come shooting out of the backpack's slot all at once. They hit Clayton in the stomach, arm, and head before tumbling to the floor.

Clayton's face turns bright red.

"Like I said, Billy. This is the part that needs a little work."

"It's a great start, Clayton," I say, bending down to help him pick up the books. "Let me know if you need any help. Keep up the good work."

I race home as usual, even though there isn't anything pressing waiting for me at the office. Then I feed Philo and we head out.

When we arrive at the World Headquarters of Sure Things, Inc. (also known as Manny's garage), I see Manny staring at his computer screen. Nothing unusual about that.

"Hey! What's going on?" I ask.

Manny doesn't say a word. He just points at the screen. He has the *Right Next Door* website open to the article on Sure Things, Inc. I start reading:

SURE THINGS, INC.
INVENTOR BILLY SURE
VS.
CFO MANNY REYES
WHO IS REALLY IN CHARGE?

by Kathy Jenkins

You know Billy Sure—the thirteen-year-old kid inventor who shocked the world with his All Ball, and later the Stink Spectacular, Gross-to-Good Powder, and No-Trouble Bubble. Now his company is coming out with some merchandise for *Alien Zombie Attack!*, the new film starring award-winning actress Gemma Weston.

But do you REALLY know Billy Sure?! Read and YOU decide!

"My company would be nothing without my Chief Financial Officer, Danny Reyes," Billy said in an EXCLUSIVE tell-all *Right Next Door* interview!

"Danny does everything for Sure Things, Inc.," he continued. "All I do is invent."

Danny Reyes—or, more accurately, as this reporter uncovered, Manny Reyes—is the CFO of Sure Things, Inc., meaning, according to Billy, "he handles the numbers, marketing, sales—really everything." All this despite the fact that Billy doesn't seem to even know his business partner's name!
Billy went on to say some more SHOCKING things about Sure Things, Inc.!!!

"Danny is responsible for all our *Alien Zombie Attack!* merchandise too," Billy said. "He took my hovercraft and made it accessible. But of course, the most important thing is that it has the Sure name on it."

When this reporter asked, "Don't you mean Manny?" Billy shrugged. "I guess," he said.

So, there you have it, folks: Sure Things, Inc. isn't just a sure thing—it's a Reyes thing too.

And if this reporter were Manny Reyes, she'd probably look for a less self-absorbed inventor to work with.

I'm absolutely stunned. This . . . this is a CRAZY BUNCH OF LIES!

"You have to know that this is all messed up," I say to Manny. "These are not my words."

"Of course," Manny says, waving off my concern. "It's completely ridiculous. Just a gimmick to gain readers. And you know what I always say . . . there's no such thing as bad press. Forget what she wrote. I'm just waiting for the bump in sales of the hovercraft toy from this nonsense."

Manny may be able to remain calm about this, but I'm really upset.

"She took everything I said out of context and twisted it. Or she just made stuff up. And you know I never tried to keep you and your contributions a secret. Just the opposite! I tried to bring you into every interview she ever did with me, but she didn't seem to want to know about you . . . until now. What could have changed? And why does she have to lie about me in the process?"

Manny stares at the article again and notices something. "What's this?" he asks, pointing to the bottom of the piece. There, in tiny type, it reads:

THIS FEATURE ARTICLE WAS SPONSORED BY DEFINITE DEVICES.

"Manny, what is DEFINITE DEVICES?" I ask.

"I don't know, but I'm going to find out," replies Manny. "I'm going to call Kathy Jenkins and get to the bottom of this!"

Chapter Three

Operation Sure Fix

THAT NIGHT AT HOME I DO MY BEST TO FOCUS ON my homework.

Except I can't concentrate. I can't believe how annoyed I am by all this. I mean, Kathy Jenkins has never accurately reported on Sure Things, Inc. She always builds me up and leaves Manny out of everything we're ever done. But this! This is a new low. This is just . . . well, a bunch of lies.

I turn back to my history book when I hear a soft knock at my door. It's probably Mom coming to make me feel better.

"Come in," I say.

But when the door swings open I see Emily standing there, holding a STEAMING MUG OF HOT CHOCOLATE and a plate full of DOUBLE-CHOCOLATE CHIP COOKIES.

"I thought a nice little snack might cheer you up," she says, putting the cup and plate down on my desk. And that's when I notice the printed-out version of Kathy's article sticking out of her back pocket. She must know I am feeling down.

"Oh," I say, unable to hide my surprise. "Thanks, Em."

I know this is all part of Emily's "doing something nice for everyone in the family" routine, but I really appreciate it. Normally, Emily is completely oblivious to my moods. She seems to not care if I'm really happy about something or upset about something, unless, of course, that something has to do with her.

I bite into a cookie as she starts to leave the room.

"It'll be okay, Billy," she says, turning

back toward me. "Everything works out for the best."

Okay, now I know she's not just being Super Nice Emily. She's ULTRA SUPER NICE EMILY. "Everything works out for the best" is one of Mom's favorite sayings, not Emily's. If I had to pick a typical Emily expression it might be something more like "Go away, genius!"

"Thanks for the snack," I say again. Then she leaves the room.

After staring at my history book for a few more minutes, I give up and go to bed. Emily's hot chocolate really hit the spot. I fall into a dreamy sleep.

I'm at the office.

"What's the latest on the marketing plan for the hovercraft toy, Danny?" I ask.

"What did you call me?" Manny shoots back.

"DANNY," I say, startled by the tone in his voice. "That's your name, isn't it?" I can't ever remember Danny getting angry. Certainly not at me. He always takes everything with an even temper. What's he getting so mad about?

"So Kathy Jenkins was right," Manny says. "You think you're so great that you can't even remember your partner's name? Well, that's it. I'm not your partner anymore. I quit!"

"What? Danny, wait," I plead.

"No, my mind is made up, *Willy*," he says. "I quit. This is the end of Sure Things, Inc. I'm giving you one hour to get all your stuff out of my garage. This partnership, this friendship is over!"

"Danny, no! No! NO!"

"Billy, wake up! Billy, honey, wake up. . . ."

I hear Mom's voice floating through the air. Suddenly Manny and the garage vanish. I open my eyes. I'm still in bed. Mom sits beside me. It was a dream. A terrible dream.

"Oh, honey, you must have had a nightmare," Mom says. "You were groaning and thrashing your arms. I just came in to wake you up for school."

"I'm so glad it was just a dream, Mom," I say, my heart still pounding. "It's all because of that stupid article."

"I know, honey, I read it," Mom says. "It was terribly unfair of Kathy, and it's some pretty despicable journalism. But I do think that Manny is right. This press, even if it isn't true, will lead to more sales for your new hovercraft toy."

"Yeah, but I feel so bad for Manny," I point out.

"Manny is too good a friend to think that you had anything to do with the stuff Kathy wrote. He knows you. He knows how much you appreciate everything he does at Sure Things, Inc. And he's your best friend."

I nod. "Thanks, Mom."

"Now get ready for school," she says, heading out of my room.

I'm feeling a little better after talking to Mom. I always do. It's been really nice having her home. Video chats just aren't the same.

When I arrive at school, I hurry down the

hall, trying not to be late for my first class. A few kids walk right past me. Some kids whisper when I walk by. Is there something wrong? Do I have some BREAKFAST BURRITO dangling from my chin?

I tap my chin but nope, no breakfast burrito. Then I pass Peter MacHale. I have to admit that Peter is not my favorite kid at school. He's very into the latest gossip and is always giving me a hard time about my inventions and TV appearances. I think Peter thinks I'm a self-obsessed celebrity or something.

As I approach Peter, I see him hunched over with a group of kids. He's got that usual goofy smile on his face and his voice is way too loud for what Principal Gilamon likes to call "HALLWAY CHATTER." He's obviously telling a story.

But as soon as Peter spots me, he stops talking and turns away from me. Instead of looking at Peter's face, I'm staring at his back! Normally, he'd try to drag me into the conversation by saying something goofy or just plain dumb. But today—nothing. Silence. And no one in his crowd even looks at me.

I continue down the hall, wondering if this is because of Kathy Jenkins's article. Did everyone read it? Does everyone now think I'm a bad guy? Nah, couldn't be, *right*?

That's when I spot Samantha Jenkins, Kathy's daughter.

Not so long ago, she used to follow me down the halls as I went from class to class.

She spots me coming toward her and instantly turns and hurries away. I know which room she's supposed to be going to right now. It's in the opposite direction from the one she's walking in. She's running away from *me*. There's no other explanation for it.

I arrive in my history class feeling frazzled. As I slip into my seat, I see Petula Brown. She has sat next to me all year in history. She's one of the most popular girls in school. We're not really friends, but she did come to my surprise birthday party, so I figure she might be a good TEST SUBJECT to find out if I'm making this all up or not.

"Hi, Petula," I say.

Her eyes narrow and she shoots me a look that makes me feel like a criminal. Then she quickly turns away.

Ms. Sullivan, my history teacher, starts her lesson. I do my best to focus, but it's not easy. I'm worrying about everyone at school hating me.

Finally Ms. Sullivan asks a question I know the answer to. My hand shoots straight up. But Ms. Sullivan keeps looking around the room. It's almost like she's avoiding me. She's looking everywhere *but* at me! Then I look around and see that no one else has a hand raised. Oh no. Does Ms. Sullivan think I'm a bad guy too?

The bell rings and I hurry along to my next class. I spot Manny in the hallway. Normally he's kind of a loner at school—he and I both prefer it that way.

But today a crowd of kids walks alongside him. Some give him sympathetic looks, others pat him on the back.

What is going on?!

Manny rounds the corner and runs into Principal Gilamon. I stop short, far enough away to not be seen, but close enough to hear their conversation.

"Manny, I was hoping to see you," says Principal Gilamon.

"Is that so?" Manny asks, sounding as if he's worried that he might be in some kind of trouble.

After all, nobody ever likes to hear the principal say *"I WAS HOPING TO SEE YOU."*

"I was wondering if you needed some more

time to complete your homework assignments," Principal Gilamon says. "We sometimes grant homework extensions when a student has an outside situation that would prevent his or her completion of homework on time."

"I'm doing fine getting my homework done, Principal Gilamon," Manny says, sounding as confused as I am feeling hearing the question. Manny always gets his homework done on time. Usually, ahead of time.

"Well, I just thought that since you are obviously doing the bulk of the work at Sure Things, Inc., you might need some extra help," Principal Gilamon explains. "And all this time I thought Billy was a role model here at Fillmore Middle. Obviously I was wrong."

"Principal Gilamon, if you're referring to that article, it was completely—"

Manny's attempt to explain away Kathy's article gets cut short when Principal Gilamon spots me. He immediately turns and walks away from Manny. But not before shooting me a NASTY GLARE!

Manny catches my eye and shakes his head. Then we both hurry off to class, where I prepare for a whole new group of kids to give me dirty looks.

After school I rush to the office. At least nobody there is going to give me a dirty look—not unless I refuse to give Philo a treat, anyway. I plop down into the chair next to Manny's desk.

"Don't worry, I have an idea to fix everything," Manny says, seeing how down I look.

Of course he does. Manny always has an idea to fix everything—reason #333 why I'm glad he's my best friend and business partner.

"Okay, what's the plan?" I ask.

"We invent something new," Manny says calmly.

"It's all part of OPERATION SURE FIX," Manny continues. "Of course, I'll keep trying to contact Kathy Jenkins, who hasn't returned any of my phone calls or e-mails. I need to do a contrasting interview to clear up the wrong information. Then I need to find out what Definite Devices is."

I nod.

"But I also think that the best publicity move we can make right now is to take attention away from this whole mess. And the best way to do that is show everyone we're still a team, with a new invention. That way people will stop focusing on all this drama."

Manny pauses and looks at me. I guess he's trying to see if I find this idea upsetting.

And I'm not sure what I *do* feel. Sad? Mad? Confused? A little bit of all three, I guess.

"I hate to put this new pressure on you, Billy, but I really think a new product would be just the thing to make people forget about that article," Manny says.

He's right. I know it.

"Operation Sure Fix for the win! Let's do it," I say. Now the idea actually makes me feel more optimistic than I have since the article came out. "I'd rather worry about inventing than about how to get people to like me again."

Then it hits me.

"Of course, now the only question is . . . what do I invent?"

Chapter Four

Now You See Me . . .

MANNY AND I THROW SOME IDEAS AROUND. LIKE revisiting the Candy Toothbrush, our first invention idea, or a Truthboard, a keyboard that will only let you type the truth (I guess you don't have to wonder where *that* inspiration came from). I was really into the idea of the Truthboard, but Manny doesn't think it will be good for authors who write about things like monsters and dragons.

At school the next day, I arrive in a pretty good mood. Even though it can be difficult, I always love coming up with a new invention.

And then I walk down the hallway.

Herman Torosian, the star of our Fillmore Falcons football team, stares at me like he's ready to tackle me against the wall. Brian Josephs, who used to be my lab partner in science class, sees me and takes off, walking quickly in the opposite direction.

Even Mike Stevenson, whose claim to fame was having the biggest booger collection in the whole school, walks past me without saying hello. Let me repeat. The BOOGER COLLEC-TOR doesn't want to have anything to do with me! How sad is that?

Don't get me wrong. I'm glad everyone is so protective of Manny that they are mad when they think I did something to hurt him. But no one is more protective of Manny than me.

Just as I'm thinking this—oh no, here comes Allison Arnolds . . . who I maybe, sort of have a crush on.

She walks past, looking right through me as if I were invisible. Great.

Allison Arnolds thinks I'm invisible.

She trots off, leaving me to my thoughts.

That's when I think.

Invisible?

INVISIBLE!

That's it! That's my idea.

When we left the set of *Alien Zombie Attack!*, Emily made a comment about being invisible. I kind of forgot about it until now. But this is it—this is the RIGHT TIME to give my full attention to inventing something that turns people invisible. It's also just the thing to take my mind off the whole *Right Next Door* mess.

And I have Allison to thank for it. Now I like her even more!

That afternoon I arrive at the office in a great mood.

"I got it, Manny!" I say, bursting into the office. Philo trots in behind me.

"What? A way to make Kathy Jenkins call me back?" Manny replies. "Because I sure haven't figured out how to make her do that."

"No, I have the idea for our next invention. INVISIBILITY!"

"That's great!" says Manny. "I love it! And today I have time to look into who is behind Definite Devices. After all, they sponsored Kathy Jenkins's article."

I get to work trying to balance the key elements in what will be my invisibility formula. I have an idea of what the formula will need. When I was at Spy Academy earlier this year with Mom, I learned about HIDDEN INK–ink that's completely undetectable until you hold it up to a light. Obviously I'll want my invisibility

46

formula to keep working under lights (and I'll want it to turn more than just ink invisible), but it's good to have as a base.

As I set up my beakers and start playing around with various combinations of liquids, I hear Manny grumbling.

"Well, I found an indie rock band call DEFINITE DEVICE, a political blog called DEFINITE DIVIDE, and a tool company selling DEFINITE DE-VICES that attach to your workbench," Manny announces. "But not a clue about what a company called DEFINITE DEVICES has to do with that article."

As the afternoon wears on, I start having better luck than Manny, which is rare. After mixing, heating, and putting a thick syruplike concoction through a small blender, I end up with a bubbling, foaming potion. Staring at it, an idea strikes me.

"Shampoo!" I cry.

"Your hair looks fine," says Manny.

"INVISIBILITY SHAMPOO," I explain. "That's how I'll make the invisibility invention

47

work! You know, lather-rinse-repeat, all of
that."

"Okay," replies Manny, always happy to
leave these kinds of inventing details to me.

I tinker with the syrupy, foaming solution
for a while longer. Then I'm ready for a test. I
pour a sample into a small plastic bottle.

"I'm heading home to test this," I say. I
grab Philo and we go back to my house.

*Lather-rinse-repeat-invisible. Lather-rinse-repeat-
invisible,* I say to myself over and over again.
At least that's what I hope it will say on the
label when we release this product. It should
make anyone who uses it invisible for an hour.

At home I walk through the front door and
Emily greets me.

"How about a nice snack?" Super Nice Emily
asks, flashing her big goofy smile. Scratch

that. I forgot she's not Super Nice Emily anymore, she's ULTRA Super Nice Emily.

"No, thanks, I have something I have to do," I say. "Shower!"

Emily glares at me, clearly disappointed I didn't want her help.

"Yeah, well, showers are something *normal humans* do everyday—" she stops herself, probably realizing that this little comment could end her deal with Dad. "Which you obviously are. SHOWER AWAY!"

I rush upstairs, grab a pair of pajamas, and head into the bathroom with my little bottle of Invisibility Shampoo. I take a shower, washing my hair with the stuff. Lather-rinse-repeat . . . and . . .

I rinse the shampoo off and look down.

IT WORKS! I am completely invisible! I can't see my legs or my feet or any of my body. I lift my hand up in front of my face. That's invisible too!

I get out of the shower and dry myself off, thrilled at my success. This is so easy to use.

It was quick to make. It's gonna be a huge hit!

When I'm all dry, I slip into my favorite footie pajamas, ones with spaceships all over them.

I step from the bathroom, heading toward my room. Meanwhile, Emily has just reached the top of the stairs.

"*AAAAAAH!*" she shrieks, pointing at me.

"What?!" I yell back, startled. "You can see me? You should *not* be able to see me! What good is an invisibility invention if you can see me?"

"Well, I can't see *you*," Emily explains. "But I can see your *footie pajamas*. They're

walking by themselves. It's really creepy!"

I look down. Emily is right. I can see my footie pajamas. I just assumed that when I put on my pajamas they would turn invisible too.

"Hold up. Billy, you invented *invisibility*. That's like, mega huge!" Emily says. "Just don't wear any clothes when you're going to be invisible. No one can see you anyway."

I think about that for a moment. On one hand it makes sense. But on the other hand . . . "That could be tough in the winter. You know, the cold weather and all."

"And, there would be another problem if you had no clothes on," Emily says.

"What's that?" I ask.

"I can see your face and hands now," Emily points out.

I lift up my hand. I can see it clearly. I look in the mirror. There's my head. "This formula was supposed to last an hour! I can't believe it wore off already!"

"So, obviously, if you are having trouble controlling exactly how long the invisibility lasts, it could get tricky if you have no clothes on."

"Yeah," I say, pretty deflated. "We don't want everyone running around in their birthday suits. Maybe I need to shower with my clothes on? But then I'd be stuck wearing wet clothes."

Hmmm ... back to the DRAWING BOARD, I guess. I'll have to tackle the refinements to my formula tomorrow at the office.

I turn to head into my bedroom when a thick rope made of colored strands all woven together comes zooming down the hallway. It floats by itself in midair.

"That's Philo's favorite dog toy!" I say. "But where's Philo?"

Emily and I look at each other, both having the same thought at the same moment.

I race to the bathroom and discover that the bottle of Invisibility Shampoo has been knocked over. A little puddle of the stuff spreads out on the floor.

"Philo must have rolled around in the spilled shampoo," I say. "You know how he loves to roll around in anything sticky or goopy."

I step from the bathroom and see a large bone bouncing past me in midair. Then the bone floats down the stairs.

Not knowing what else to do, Emily and I follow the bone down the stairs. It floats right into the living room where Mom and Dad are sitting. Dad is on his tablet. Mom is reading a magazine, happily cut off from her work for a few minutes.

"What's going on, Billy?" she asks, her head turning to follow the floating bone.

"Invisibility Shampoo," I explain.

"Makes sense," Mom says. "It was either that or a ghost, but you never know with your inventions."

At that moment, Philo reappears, completely visible now, in the living room. He happily chomps at the bone in his mouth.

"Well, yeah, but it obviously needs some more work," I say, patting Philo on the head. Then I head back upstairs. Now to perfect the invisibility formula. . . .

Chapter Five

Lather, Rinse . . . and Repeat

THE NEXT MORNING AT SCHOOL, I RECEIVE THE SAME treatment I've gotten for the last few days. Kids look away from me, turn and walk in the opposite direction from me, or shoot me nasty looks.

But today, none of it bothers me—at least not as much. Maybe I'm just getting used to it, but really, I think it's because I'm now working on a new invention. I'm always at my HAPPIEST when I'm plugging away on a new idea!

I spend the whole day thinking about the

Invisibility Shampoo. Then I grab Philo and head over to the office, where I find Manny looking concerned.

"Operation Sure Fix is off to a slow start. I still haven't heard back from Kathy Jenkins," he explains. "I'm starting to think that she *wanted* to spread lies about Sure Things, Inc."

"It does seem that way, huh?" I say.

"It does," Manny agrees. "And it just doesn't make sense. First Kathy Jenkins loves Sure Things, Inc. Then we become *more* successful, and now she doesn't? Something happened . . . I'm willing to bet this has something to do with Definite Devices."

"What do you mean?" I ask.

"Definite Devices sponsored Kathy's articles, so I think they paid her to write lies about us. Now we just have to figure it out—who and what is DEFINITE DEVICES? They've sure done a good job keeping themselves invisible. I can't find a thing about them."

Manny is right, but I don't know what to say about Definite Devices now.

"Speaking of invisible . . ." I say, changing the subject.

"Oh, yeah, how'd the shampoo work?" Manny asks.

I fill Manny in on the half-successful trial run. "I think Philo liked it best of all."

"URRRRRRR." Philo moans at the mention of his name. He's sitting upright in his doggy bed, ears standing straight up. I know this pose. He's on high alert. Just because I mentioned his name?

That's weird. Usually he'll only go full-on high alert if another person enters the room. But after a few seconds he lies back down in his bed.

"Well, here's some good news," Manny says. I come over and look at his screen.

"This is our marketing plan for the hover-craft toy," he begins. "It'll be in every major toy chain by the end of the year! And the app is already available for smartphones. You can fly a virtual hovercraft on your phone, but once the actual item becomes available, the app will transition into a great MARKETING TOOL to help sell the toy."

"Nice," I say. I don't know much about marketing, but I'm always impressed by how good at this stuff Manny is.

"And here is the plan for some other hovercraft-related merchandise," he contin-ues. "Let's see, we've got a hovercraft-shaped lunchbox, a hovercraft-shaped key chain, a poster that's shaped like the hovercraft . . . oh, and look at this one, a waffle maker shaped like the hovercraft."

"People want hovercraft-shaped waffles?" I ask.

"Take a look at the advance order numbers and decide for yourself."

I scroll down Manny's spreadsheet.

"Wow!" I nearly yell in disbelief. "Manny, you're a genius!"

I get back to my workbench and start again with the ingredients for the Invisibility Shampoo. But this time I change the amounts, heat them up in a different order, and combine them more slowly.

A short while later, I'm ready to test the new version.

"Rather than waiting until I go home again tonight, I'm going to test it right here," I tell Manny.

"How're you gonna do that?" he asks.

"In the sink," I say. "I figure that if I shampoo my hair with my clothes on, my whole body and all my clothes should disappear."

Many nods and goes back to his spreadsheet.

I bring a small dish of my new Invisibility

Shampoo over to a sink in the corner of the garage. Manny's dad put this sink in when he built the garage, figuring that he'd be using the garage as his workshop. Little did he know that Sure Things, Inc. would come along and change all those plans! Now we mostly use the sink when we wash our hands after eating pizza from the custom pizza-maker.

I turn on the faucet and wait for the water to get warm. Then I stick my head under the running water. It feels KIND OF SILLY—I've

had my head stuck under sinks when I've gotten haircuts, but no one told me how hard it is to do yourself! I get water all over my neck and down my shirt. This must be what Emily felt like after washing the car.

When my hair is good and wet, I pour some of the shampoo onto it, scrubbing. Thick white foamy bubbles form. I work it all through my hair, deciding that I should let the shampoo sit in my hair for a little bit before washing it out.

I stand up and the white soapy suds drip down onto my shirt.

Philo looks up at my white foamy hair and tilts his head in confusion.

"It's okay, boy. It's just me."

Then suddenly Philo stands up, steps from his bed, and stares at an empty corner of the office. He starts growling!

"GRRRRR . . . GRRRRRR . . ."

"What is wrong with you, Philo?" I ask.

"RUFF . . . RUFF!!"

Now he's barking at nothing.

"Philo, be quiet! There's nothing there!"

But he continues to stare into the corner and growl menacingly . . . or at least what passes as menacingly for Philo.

I wait a few more minutes, then go back to the sink. I stick my head under the running water and rinse out all the shampoo.

Manny looks over at me and his eyes open wide. I know him well enough to see that he is trying to hold back a giggle.

Meanwhile, Philo takes one look at me, whimpers, then turns back to barking at the empty corner.

"What?" I ask. "Didn't it work?"

Before Manny can say anything, I look at my hands. I can plainly see both of them. I glance down. My soaking wet shirt is also visible.

"So it didn't work at all!"

"Well, I wouldn't say that, exactly." Manny replies, giggling. "Take a look in the mirror."

I go over to a mirror hanging on the wall. Peering at my reflection, I step back in shock. The only thing that has turned invisible is my HAIR!

"Oh great!" I moan. "I can see my scalp!"

"Think of it as a preview of what you might look like when you're bald," Manny says, unable to hold back another round of uncontrollable giggling. "On the bright side, I think you've figured out next year's Halloween costume."

"Yeah, yeah, very funny. Looks like I'm back to the drawing board yet again."

So, sitting back at my workbench, with my bald head, I go back to work. It's obvious that shampoo is not going to work as an invisibility delivery system. I need something that can spray all over my body and clothes . . . WAIT A MINUTE. That's it.

"I think I have it, Manny," I say.

"Uh-huh," he says without turning around to look at me. I'm guessing that at this point he can't look at my bald head without cracking up, and he doesn't want to make me feel any worse than I already do.

"Forget shampoo," I say. "I'm going to work on an INVISIBILITY SPRAY. It will be quicker and easier, plus you can spray yourself and your clothes all over without getting soaking wet!"

Just as I say that, there's a noise behind me. I spin around and see Manny's cat, Watson, rolling around. Watson doesn't come much to the garage, so I'm not used to him being here, although he and Philo get along well (more like they ignore each other). Still, the noise sounded like someone gasping . . . oh well. There's no one else but Watson there, so it must have been him.

Chapter Six

Help Wanted

I GET BACK TO MY BENCH TO WORK ON THE INVISIBILITY Spray. I have got to figure out how to make this invisibility formula work the way I want it to work. The future of Sure Things, Inc.—not to mention my REPUTATION—is at stake!

Manny continues to plug away on his marketing plans.

"You know what I could really go for now?" Manny asks.

"An invisibility invention that actually works?" I reply.

"Well, sure, but I have no doubt you'll

get there, Billy," Manny says. "But I could totally go for a QUESADILLA. Mmm, all that cheese."

"I know what you mean," I say, although I think if Manny wants something cheesy, he should just help himself to some pizza from the office's pizza machine. Don't get me wrong—quesadillas taste delicious. I'm just not sure Manny is about to leave the office, go to a Mexican restaurant, and order one while Operation Sure Fix is in full investigation mode.

I look down at my Invisibility Spray formula, testing different kinds of heat and ways to mix it. When it's less goopy than the shampoo, and thinner, like vegetable oil, I decide it's ready.

Time to test it!

Here goes . . .

I put the formula in a spray bottle, squeeze the handle, and spritz the top of my workbench with it.

I wait . . . and wait . . . and wait some more.

But NOTHING HAPPENS. My workbench is still visible.

After three more tweaks with no success, I realize that it's getting late, and I need to go home.

"I'm not having too much luck here, Manny," I say. "Which means it's time to sleep-invent! With any luck I'll have something useful in the morning."

Okay, okay, I know sleep-inventing sounds weird, but it's what I do. Whenever I'm close to cracking the code on an invention, but can't quite get it when I'm awake, I go to sleep with a pen under my pillow and wake up to fully rendered blueprints.

"Have a good night," Manny says. "And by

the way, thanks, Billy. I didn't even hear you leave and come back."

"What are you talking about?" I ask. "I've been here working away the whole time."

"I'm talking about this!" Manny says. "This EXTRA-DELICIOUS, EXTRA-CHEESY quesadilla!"

I turn around and see Manny holding up a quesadilla, which he has just taken a big bite out of.

Okay, now I'm really confused and a little creeped out.

"Um, Manny, I didn't get you that quesadilla," I say.

"Hmm. . . ." Manny replies, unfazed as usual. "Maybe one of my parents brought it in and I didn't notice."

"That makes sense. Or maybe Ultra Super Nice Emily got it and snuck it in here. Anyway, enjoy. I'm outta here. Wish me luck sleep-inventing tonight."

"Grood luurck," Manny says through a mouthful of quesadilla.

A short while later Philo and I arrive at home. Once again, Emily is right there at the door to greet me. I'm starting to feel like I have a butler.

"How was your day, DEAREST BROTHER?" asks Emily, handing me yet another plate of double-chocolate chip cookies.

The cookies are great. Emily . . . well, like I said, all this niceness is getting to be a little much.

"Okay," I say. "Although I'm still having a little trouble nailing down my latest invention."

"Well, I'm sure it will all work out," she says, flashing that weird smile she seems to have perfected.

I look over Emily's shoulder into the kitchen and spot Mom. She rolls her eyes in sympathy. Obviously Emily overdoing the nice thing weirds her out as much as it does me.

"What do you think of this one, Billy?" Dad says, carrying a large painting in from the living room. "I just finished it. It should be the final piece for my show."

I stare at the canvas. It looks like a long white spear hanging down from the roof of a cave.

"A stalactite?" I ask. "We studied those in science class."

"No, silly. It's a close-up of one of PHILO'S UPPER TEETH," Dad says, beaming with pride.

"That was definitely my second guess," I say, smiling.

Later, at dinner, Dad is in such a good mood

that he insists on cooking. Which, well . . . kind of puts *us* in a bad mood.

"Okeydokey, here we go," says Dad, gripping a steaming casserole dish. "Tuna Hot Dog Spaghetti supreme! Everyone's favorite meals, all in one dish!"

"Lovely, dear," says Mom. Then: "Emily, honey, can you please pass the salt?"

Emily grabs the salt and passes it over. Only Dad doesn't know it's actually Gross-to-Good Powder which makes his dishes edible.

After dinner I grab what's left of my plate of cookies and head to my room. There's an e-mail waiting from Manny.

Still nothing from Kathy Jenkins. No e-mail, no returned phone calls. Also no closer to figuring out what Definite Devices is. Knocking off for the evening. Sleep well . . . but not too well!!

—M

It's nice of Manny to wish me luck with my sleep-inventing. I always get a little nervous trying to fall asleep knowing that I need to get up in the middle of the night, sit at my desk, and crank out blueprints that solve the problems. Yet, somehow, it usually works.

Before getting into bed, I go through my usual routine of setting up a blank piece of blueprint paper on my desk and putting my favorite drawing pen under my pillow.

As usual, on a night when I know I have to sleep-invent, I have trouble falling asleep. I toss and turn for a while before dozing off.

Eventually I fall into a restless dream in which all the kids in my school are marching outside the headquarters of Sure Things, Inc.

Allison Arnolds is leading them all. There are signs that are all pro-Manny and anti-Billy.

I turn to Manny to make sure that he is still not upset with me, but he has turned into a giant quesadilla with arms, legs, and a huge hot pepper for a head!

Which is when I realize that I must be DREAMING, and the crazy images melt away.

I jump from bed and rush to my desk. Did I do it? Did I sleep-invent?

SUCCESS!!

I sit at my desk and look over the wide sheet of blueprint paper. The first thing I feel

is relief, then I feel really, really happy. It's official. I officially have fully rendered blueprints for the Invisibility Spray!

I look over the plans in detail. *Bacon is the main ingredient,* I think. *Hmm. I would have never thought of that while I was awake.* But looking at how it works together with the other ingredients and the spray delivery system on these blueprints, it makes perfect sense.

As I start to roll up the blueprints, I notice something weird—there's *another* set of blueprints underneath it! This one is for an ANTI-INVISIBILITY SPRAY. Apparently I had a busy night of sleep-inventing. But, of course, that makes perfect sense. With the two sprays it's up to you exactly how long you want to remain invisible. You can turn yourself visible again whenever you want!

I bet this could be way useful for Mom on one of her super-secret spy missions!

And speaking of Mom, when I head downstairs for breakfast I see that she has beaten Dad to the stove, meaning that *she* gets to cook breakfast!

"Whatcha making, Mom?" I ask, settling into my chair in a great mood. I'm thinking my great mood can even rival Ultra Super Nice Emily's. At least mine is real!

"Well, since your father is in the final stages of getting ready for his art show, I decided to make us breakfast," Mom says. "It's just pancakes. PLAIN, OLD, NORMAL, BORING PANCAKES from a mix."

Mom smiles at me. After years of eating Dad's breakfasts—like olive-and-gravy omelets, or salmon cereal—plain, old, boring pancakes sound great.

"Perfect," I say.

Emily sits down next to me. She gives

me a weird look. As she snatches a couple of pancakes from the platter, I can see there's something wrong. This is certainly not "happy to help you" Emily, but somehow I can tell it also isn't "this is about me, right? Because it's always all about me" Emily. Something is really troubling her.

"Good morning?" I say, not meaning for it to sound as much like a question as it does. I guess I don't know how to react to CONCERNED EMILY.

"Take a look at this," Emily says, pulling out her phone. "I think you need to see it, though you're not going to like it."

Oh no. Emily brings up the mobile version of *Right Next Door* on her phone. She scrolls to today's classified ad section.

With a mouth stuffed full of Mom's pancakes, I read:

DEFINITE DEVICES JOB OPENING
Seeking a CFO for a new invention
company. Must have prior experience

at an invention company. Come work for a NICE boss! ALWAYS gives credit! ALWAYS remembers your name! Will be your FRIEND first, and your BUSINESS PARTNER second! Definite Devices is MORE THAN SURE—we're DEFINITE! Please contact Nat Definite for all inquiries.

The posting goes on to list Nat Definite's e-mail address.

"It's pretty obvious this Nat Definite wants *your* CFO to apply for this position, Billy," Emily says very seriously. "The good news is, at least you have a name and an e-mail address for Definite Devices now, right?"

She's not wrong, but it's hard for me to picture any bright side to this situation.

Then, making sure that Mom is in earshot, ULTRA SUPER NICE EMILY says, "If you need help finding out who Nat Definite is, let me know! I'm a pretty good sleuth, ya know!" she says.

Whatever is left of my good mood is now completely gone. I'm worried. I can't lose Manny! Manny is my best friend! Not to mention, there is no Sure Things, Inc. without him . . . and despite what everyone else thinks, no one knows that better than me!

Why is Nat Definite trying to steal my CFO?

Chapter Seven

Definite Trouble

I GRAB MY PHONE AND SHOOT OFF A TEXT TO MANNY.

> Did you see today's Right Next Door? Check
> out their classified ads. It looks like Definite
> Devices is trying to recruit you . . .

Now, I know and trust Manny. There's just
about no one I trust as much. After all, we
were best friends long before we became business partners. But this obvious, direct attempt
to steal Manny away still has me worried. If
Manny really wants to—

Ping!

My phone sounds, letting me know that Manny has instantly replied to my text.

> No worries, partner, I do NOT want to move to another company. I do NOT want to work with anyone other than you. This seems fishy. Like it was written just for me. I'm suspicious.

I leave the house and head to school. My mood is picking up a bit. I've got the blueprints for the Invisibility and the Anti-Invisibility Sprays rolled up and in my backpack. I now feel confident that no matter what, Manny will ALWAYS be my partner.

And then I arrive at school.

I'm used to no one paying any attention to me as I walk through the halls these days. But something is different today. There are crowds of kids gathered in small circles chatting excitedly.

As I walk past groups of kids, I catch snippets of their conversation.

"No way," says Allison Arnolds.

"Way," says Judy Geralds.

"You actually eat the book?"

"Uh-huh, that's why they call it an EDIBLE BOOK!" shouts another kid.

"Yeah, it's from Definite Devices. They're new," says an eighth grader.

Definite Devices? This last statement stops me in my tracks. Did Definite Devices release its first invention?

I continue down the hall. I see Petula Brown in front of a group of sixth graders who are glued to her every word.

"I know. It's amazing, isn't it?" she says. "It's their first product—the Edible Book. Instead of studying for hours, you simply *chew* the book, and instantly know everything that's written in there! It's like the information is magically put right into your brain. Cool, right?"

The sixth graders all nod in agreement. I'm not sure if they really understand what Petula is explaining, or they are just amazed that an older popular girl is interested in talking with them.

Edible Books, huh? That's actually a pretty good idea. Why didn't I think of it?

But Petula Brown isn't done yet.

"I love this invention!" she squeals. "And I bet that Definite Devices is way better—and *nicer*—than Sure Things, Inc. will ever be!"

Okay, *that* I did not need to hear.

And that's when it hits me. Definite Devices is a REAL company. And they are REAL inventors. And they have a new, REAL product out that every REAL kid at the very REAL Fillmore Middle School seems to love.

And all of that is a REAL problem if they are trying to steal Manny!

Briiiing! The bell rings and I have no choice but to head to class—history again. Kids arrive and slip into their seats. As I open up my textbook, I see three kids chewing on books from their bags.

Riiip!

They tear pages out of their books.

Crumple, crumple, crumple. . . .

They crumple up the pages into little balls.

Chomp, chomp, smack!

They shove the crumpled pages into their mouths and chew . . . on paper! That is so gross!

Or is it?

"Mine tastes like blueberry pie," says one girl.

"Mine tastes like a chocolate milkshake," says a boy sitting next to her.

"Yum. French fries with ketchup," says another girl as she swallows a page. She pauses for a moment, then turns around to face the rest of the class.

"Did you know that President Thomas Jefferson greeted guests at the White House in his bathrobe and slippers?" says the french fry girl.

"Oh yeah?" says the milkshake boy. "Well, did you know that in New Jersey in 1820, a basket of tomatoes was put on trial for being evil?"

Okay, I didn't know that.

Blueberry pie girl chimes in next. "Did you know that Cleopatra lived closer in time to the invention of the smartphone than she did to the building of the Great Pyramid?"

Um, I didn't know that either. Definite Devices may be onto something here. I'm getting **VERY NERVOUS** about this now. And that's when Ms. Sullivan walks in.

"Excuse me, Harry," she says to a boy who has just shoved a crumpled-up page from his Edible Book into his mouth. "Why are you **EATING YOUR TEXTBOOK?**"

"Rits ra rediba ook," Harry mumbles.

"Excuse me, Harry, but I can't understand you with your mouth full of paper," Ms. Sullivan says.

Harry reaches into his mouth and pulls out a disgusting, drippy, half-chewed wad of paper. "It's an Edible Book, Ms. Sullivan. I can eat it instead of reading it."

"Yes, well, that's very nice, Harry, but in this class we *read* our books," Ms. Sullivan says. "You may eat whatever you like at lunchtime."

Okay, so I can see how Edible Books are

going to be way more popular with kids than with teachers.

The kids in history class who have Edible Books quickly slip them into their bags and pull out their regular textbooks.

My next class is science. And again, when I walk into the classroom I see about five kids ripping pages from their books and shoving the paper into their mouths.

I can't wait for Mr. Palnacchio, my science teacher, to see this. He's a pretty serious, by-the-book kind of teacher. And by "by-the-book," I mean the kind of book you have to read.

"Check this out," says Brian Josephs. "A flea can jump one hundred and thirty times its own height. If a person could do that, he would be able to jump seven hundred and eighty feet into the air."

"I got one," says Mary Jane Murphy. "If you farted nonstop for six years, you would create enough energy to destroy a building!"

"Well, you'd certainly empty the building,

that's for sure," Mike Stevenson adds. He tears out a page and shoves it into his mouth. "But check this out. The tentacles of a giant Arctic jellyfish can grow to one hundred and twenty feet long!"

A girl named Stella goes next. "Cats can make over a hundred different vocal sounds. Dogs can only make about ten. I think my cat Loafer can make about a million."

Judy Geralds eats a page and then announces, "Did you know that three percent of the ice in the Antarctic is made up of penguin pee?"

"Actually, that's just a myth, Ms. Geralds," says Mr. Palnacchio as he steps into the room. "Don't believe everything you read."

Or in this case, everything you EAT!

Mr. Palnacchio starts writing today's lesson on the board. Just before I start to copy it down, I shoot off a quick text to Manny.

Lunch today? It's important.

Manny and I rarely have lunch together at school. We try hard to hang out with other friends at school since we see each other every day at the Sure Things, Inc. office. But this is different. So much has happened—and so quickly—since I saw Manny at the office yesterday. I really need to catch up with him.

A few seconds later I get a return text.

Sounds good. See you then.

Lunch finally rolls around. As I walk into the cafeteria, I'm happy to see kids eating something other than their books. I spot Manny at a table across the room. Filling up my tray with a burger, a salad, and some kinda scary-looking dish called fruit surprise, (where's the Gross-to-Good Powder when you need it?) I join him.

"What's up?" Manny asks as he pokes his fruit surprise with a fork and gives it a skeptical look.

"Well, the good news is I had a great night of sleep-inventing," I say, figuring it's always better to start with the good news. "Not only did I work out the kinks for the Invisibility Spray, but as a bonus, I also came up with blueprints for an Anti-Invisibility Spray, too. That way you can turn invisible and turn back any time you want."

"THAT'S FANTASTIC!" Manny says, deciding to shove aside his fruit surprise in favor of his burger. "But that's not all we need to talk about."

"Obviously that job listing is very bad," I say. "Definite Devices is becoming a real problem.

And now they've come out with Edible Books. I'm sure you've seen them." Manny nods. "They prove that Definite Devices is a real company and that they can invent a popular product. *And* they can get it to market very quickly!"

"The Edible Books *are* a neat idea," Manny concedes.

"I wish I'd thought of it," I say.

But Manny shakes his head. "I would have fought you on bringing that one to market, partner," he says. "It's one thing to get *kids* to like an invention, but quite another one to get parents and teachers to buy into it. And I just don't see teachers going gaga for this. It sounds to me like Definite Devices really does need a good CFO. Long term, I predict a FAILURE in the marketplace."

Even though I was kinda jealous of the idea at first, based on my teachers' reactions, I'd have to say that Manny is probably right. Sometimes he's really good at being the grown-up. Scary good, in fact, for a kid who's exactly my age.

Reason #998 that I'm super glad Manny is my business partner.

"But what about that job listing?" I ask.

"That was obviously written for me," says Manny. "It was designed to lure me over to Definite Devices."

"So what's next for Operation Sure Fix?" I ask.

"We have to find out who Nat Definite at Definite Devices is," Manny says. "I think I have a plan that will work."

I always love it when Manny has a plan. I start to feel encouraged. "What's the plan?"

"Okay," Manny says. "Here it is. There's really no other way."

Manny looks at me.

"I need to infiltrate Definite Devices," he continues. "I have to go on the inside, find out who Nat Definite is, gain Nat's trust, figure out what's going on, and learn how to stop him." Manny pauses. "And for that, I'm going to have to apply for that job."

90

Chapter Eight

Caution—Inventor at Work!

WORST FEAR: CONFIRMED!

I don't know. I just don't know. I mean,
I know Manny isn't *actually* applying for the
job. On the one hand, it makes perfect sense.
What better way is there to gain inside intel
about Definite Devices than by actually having
someone on the inside?

But on the other hand, the idea of Manny
working for another company . . . even *pretend-
ing* to work for another company . . . that idea
is still just TOO WEIRD.

"Billy? You okay?" Manny says after a few

seconds. "You look like you left the planet for moment there."

"What? Oh, sorry, I guess I got lost in my thoughts." I think for a few more seconds. I know Manny isn't about to leave Sure Things, Inc. I know this is for us. "Yeah, let's go for it," I say, logic winning out over worry. "We've got to find out what's going on, and getting you on the inside of Definite Devices seems like a perfect way."

Manny nods, then decides to abandon the fruit surprise altogether.

"Just don't get too comfortable there!" I say.

Manny raises his eyebrows.

"I know . . . I know . . . it's just a SPY MIS-SION," I say. "But really, Manny, you're my best friend. I'm always happy to have you on my team."

Manny nods, smiling. "I feel the same way, partner," he says.

The rest of the school day is pretty uneventful. In fact, at each class I go to, every kid who eats an Edible Book is told by the teacher to put it away. Manny is right. There's no way teachers will allow these books to replace the real ones. PHEW!

That afternoon at the office I get set up to create my Invisibility Spray with the blueprints.

Glancing back over my shoulder I see Manny, fully absorbed in his laptop. I know he's busy applying for the Definite Devices CFO job. I try not to think about it too much and instead focus on my own task.

Still surprised that bacon, of all things, is an important ingredient in the Invisibility Spray, I fire up my Bunsen burner and start to cook up a load of bacon.

Tssss! As the bacon begins to sizzle, Philo hops out of his doggy bed and trots over. He

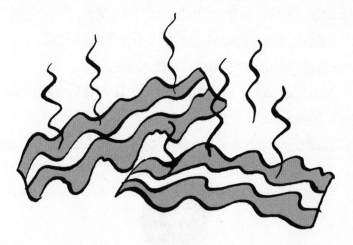

paces back and forth in front of my work-bench, sniffing and groaning.

Before I can tell him that the bacon is not for him (not that he'd care even if he understood what I was saying—where is my CAT-DOG TRANSLATOR, anyway?), Philo whips his head around and starts growling.

"What do you see, boy?" I say, looking in the direction Philo is facing. Still nothing there.

Then, just as quickly, Philo turns back and starts sniffing at the bacon.

"Sorry, boy, this bacon is not—"

And again, Philo turns around quickly and growls.

"What is up with you?!" I ask.

Philo turns back to the bacon.

"No," I say firmly. I always feel bad when I deny Philo something he wants. Especially food, but this bacon is not for breakfast. It's a key ingredient in my invention.

Still, I can't argue with Philo—it does smell pretty good.

Philo returns to his doggy bed and I start

blending small strips of bacon with the rest of my invisibility formula. When the strange brew has cooked (and my clothes smell like bacon), I'm ready to test my spray.

But not before Philo hops from his bed, races to a corner of the office, and starts barking. "THERE'S NOTHING THERE, PHILO!" I say. What is wrong with my dog?! It looks like his bacon craving has made him a little wacky.

Then, just as quickly as he started, Philo stops, pauses at my workbench to beg for bacon again, and returns to his bed.

Sometimes I think that I will never understand dogs.

Time to test my spray. I line up a water bottle, a book, and a small electric motor. I spray a small amount on each of these items, and accidentally get a little of the spray on my left arm.

Then I wait . . . and wait . . . probably only a few seconds, but to me, after my previous failures, it feels like hours! And then the water bottle, the book, and motor start to disappear.

It's working! I think, as half of each item vanishes.

Come on, come on . . . here we go. . . .

I wait for the rest of each object to disappear. But it just doesn't happen. So here I am with a bottle, a book, and motor that are each HALF-INVISIBLE.

And that's when I glance down at my left arm. My elbow has vanished! I can see my upper arm and my shoulder, as well as my lower arm, wrist, and hand. But at the moment these two parts of my arm appear to be DISCONNECTED!

I gather up the three half-visible objects in my partially visible arms and cross the office to show Manny. As I arrive at his desk, Manny is clicking the send button on the online application for the Definite Devices CFO job.

"Well, I applied," he says, his back still facing me. "Now let's see how long it takes Nat to reply."

Manny turns around. "That's a promising

start," he says, looking at the results of my Invisibility Spray.

That's my friend Manny, always the optimist.

"I have to say, the invisible elbow thing is a bit creepy," he adds.

"Yup," is all I can think of to say. Then I notice something weird on Manny's desk. "Hey, did you move that photo of us from the time we were on the *Better Than Sleeping!* TV show? You always keep it right there on your desk, but it's gone."

I know how proud Manny is of that photo, which shows our first big brush with fame. He looks over to the spot on his desk where the photo usually sits. It's empty.

"No, I didn't move it," he says. "I don't know what could have happened to it."

Manny sticks his head under the table, checking to see if maybe the photo fell on the floor. Nope. It's nowhere to be seen.

"Well, that's weird," Manny says, then turns back to his laptop.

I fire up the burners and start cooking a new batch of bacon. I have to get busy fine-tuning my formula. As the bacon sizzles, Philo again comes over, sniffs, and groans. Then he quickly turns.

"RUUFF RUFFF!"

He starts barking again into an empty corner of the office.

I shake my head. Too many weird things going on around here.

When the bacon is done, I combine the bigger pieces with the rest of the ingredients, which include moss I scraped off a rock, rust from one of Dad's old hubcaps (or maybe it was one of his old sculptures . . . he'll never miss it either way), as well as the cream cheese, toothpaste, dried seaweed, and toenail clippings I began with.

Well, here goes, I think.

I spray the bottle, book, and motor. The visible parts now disappear.

YES! IT WORKS! I spray my left shoulder and my left wrist. Both turn invisible! I'm so happy the spray works that I start spraying my hair, my shirt, my pants, and my shoes. In a few seconds I'm completely invisible.

"It works, Manny!" I cry. "It works!"

Manny turns and stares at the spot where he heard my voice coming from. "I can't see you at all, Billy! That's fantastic!"

Intrigued, Philo steps from his bed and walks slowly over to me, sniffing as he goes.

"It's okay, boy," I say. "It's me."

I walk around the room, and Philo follows me step for step.

"You think dogs can see invisible people?" Manny asks.

And that's when it hits me. "No, but they can sure smell bacon! That has to be it. The only downside of my Invisibility Spray is that it does kinda make you smell like bacon."

"**URRRRR** . . ." Philo moans.

"So, how long does the invisibility last?" Manny asks.

I stop in my tracks. It's at that moment that I realize that I have absolutely no idea how long I will remain invisible.

"Um, actually, I don't really know," I admit.

"Is the Anti-Invisibility Spray ready?" Manny asks.

Another good question. And once again, it is not until Manny asks the question that I realize that it probably would have been a really good idea to have created the Anti-Invisibility Spray *before* I tested the Invisibility Spray on myself.

"Um, no," I admit, slightly embarrassed. "I should work on that now."

"Definitely," Manny says. "By the way, it's freaky watching you move things around when you're invisible."

Poor Manny—he probably sees a bunch of flying objects!

I get to work, following the steps to create the formula.

I start to think about the fun ways I could use this spray. Trick-or-treating on Halloween. No one would see me! They'd only see a bag of candy floating in the air with no one holding it. And I wouldn't have to worry about a costume. If only Halloween weren't months away. . . .

Thankfully it doesn't take me long to whip up a batch of Anti-Invisibility Spray. I spray the surface of the workbench to make sure I get the bottle, book, and motor—because, of course, I can't see exactly where they are. All three objects instantly come back into view.

I then turn the can toward myself and spray. I look down at my hands. A few seconds later they come back into view. Then the rest of my body becomes visible too.

"I got it!" I say. "And on the first try, too!"

Manny turns and looks at me. "That's great," he says. "But what's NOT SO GREAT is that Nat Definite has not replied to my application. I thought for sure that since that listing appeared to be written for me, he'd jump right on my application."

"You know, Emily did volunteer to help track down Nat Definite," I point out. "And even if she is only offering because it would count as an 'Emily being nice' thing, she *is* pretty good at searching the Internet."

"Worth a try," says Manny. "I'm certainly not having any luck."

I grab the phone and call Emily. "So, remember when you offered to help us find that Nat Definite guy? Well, we need—"

"I'D LOVE TO HELP!" Emily screams into the phone, not even letting me finish my sentence and causing me to pull the phone far away from my ear. "As long as this counts as a nice thing I'm doing for you."

"Yes, it counts, Emily. I—"

Too late. She hangs up. A couple minutes later—**Screeee!**—I hear her bike screeching to a halt outside.

"Hi, guys, help is here," Emily says, pulling up a chair next to Manny.

As I clean up the leftover bits and pieces of bacon and toenails, Emily and Manny put their mad geek skills to work, scouring the Internet for Nat Definite.

I'm just about done when I find a couple of extra pieces of bacon I had missed. Oh, what the heck. He's been so good. "Philoooooooo," I whisper. "Bacon."

Philo bolts from his bed as if he'd been fired from a slingshot and races over. He gobbles down the bacon right from my hand.

An hour passes and it's soon time to head home. Emily works hard, using all the tricks she knows to figure out if Nat Definite is a fake name or not, but despite her best efforts, she has no more luck than Manny has had.

"Sorry, guys, I really did try," Emily says as we head out of the office. "Let me know if you hear back from Definite Devices, Manny."

He nods, then turns back to his laptop.

Emily is in a bright, bubbly mood as she and I ride our bikes home, side by side. Philo trots happily behind us, still licking his lips, trying to get the last bits of bacony goodness.

"I already helped Mom with a project, organizing some of her files," Emily says. "And now I just helped you—even though we didn't find what we were looking for. So now I only have to do one more nice big thing for Dad and then I'm all set. I'm so close. I'm ALMOST FREE!"

Oh joy. I can hardly wait to get old Emily back.

I sleep well that night, satisfied that at least Sure Things, Inc.'s Next Big Thing is ready to go. The next day is Saturday. I look forward to sleeping a little late.

No such luck.

My phone rings early. It's Manny.

"Are you up?" he asks.

"I am now," I reply groggily.

"You have to check out *Right Next Door*," he says, offering no apology for waking me up early on a Saturday morning.

Before it can dawn on me that Manny would not be calling so early on a Saturday unless it was important, I open my laptop and click on the *Right Next Door* site.

There I am greeted by the following eye-opening headline:

DEFINITE DEVICES ANNOUNCES INVISIBILITY CREAM!

Chapter Nine

The Stranger in the Corner

I REALLY CAN'T BELIEVE THIS! I MEAN, MANNY, Emily, and I can't even figure out *who* is behind Definite Devices, and meanwhile they have already:

- introduced a popular product, the Edible Book, even though Manny is probably right about it not lasting
- done their best to steal Manny away from Sure Things, Inc.
- and now, beat us to the market with an invisibility product!

I *just* got my spray prototypes to work,

which means we'll need to safety test it and get it for stores, and they've already gone public with their INVISIBILITY CREAM! How is this even possible?!

"Um, Billy, are you there?" Manny says into the phone.

That's when I realize I'm so stunned that I haven't said a word to Manny since I saw that headline.

"Sorry, the headline really got me," I say. "Let me read the article."

Here's what it says:

Want to be invisible like a superhero or a ghost? WANT NO MORE! From the BRILLIANT and FRIENDLY mind of Nat Definite comes Definite Devices' BEST INVENTION EVER—Invisibility Cream! Did you like the Edible Book? Well, you're gonna LOVE Definite Devices' Invisibility Cream. Rub it on...and vanish from sight! Sound good? It is good! And, it's coming soon to a store near you!

Definite Devices—We're More Than
Sure. We're Definite!

I'm still stunned. And, strangely, a little jealous. Who's going to care about our Invisibility Spray when their cream is just about to hit the stores?

"Uh, Billy, did you finish the article?" Manny asks.

Once again I forgot I was even talking to him.

"Sorry, sorry . . . I don't even know what to say."

"Well, before you say anything, let me tell you . . . that article is not all," Manny says. "I have some more news. . . ."

"Okay," I say, feeling a knot tightening in my stomach.

"Nat Definite finally e-mailed me back," Manny explains. "He took the bait. He accepted my application to be Definite Devices' new CFO."

"That's great!" I say. "Now you can finally learn who he is and what his business operation looks like. This is what we've been waiting for."

"Well, um, not exactly," Manny says. "Nat asked to meet with me today, but he wants to meet at the World Headquarters of Sure Things, Inc."

This whole thing just keeps getting WEIRDER AND WEIRDER.

"What?" I reply. "Doesn't this Nat guy have his own office? I mean, he's trying to be big time, beat us out and all, and he doesn't even have his own *office*? I thought we were going to find out about him. Now *he's* going to find out about *us*!"

"I'm with you, partner," says Manny, "but he insisted. He would only agree to interview me if he could come over to our headquarters."

"Do you think it's even worth it to meet with him?" I ask. "Since you're not infiltrating yet or anything."

"Yeah, getting some face time is important," Manny says. "I'll do my best to learn everything I can about him and try to figure out what he really wants, even if I have to do it in our own office."

And that's when it hits me. A plan.

"I have an idea," I say. "What if I spray myself with the Invisibility Spray before Nat gets there? I can hide in the office and spy on him, just as he's spying on us!"

Manny thinks for a second. "I like it," he says finally. "Think of it as a new PRODUCT FIELD TEST for the Invisibility Spray. Think you can get this plan in motion ASAP? Nat is coming by at two this afternoon."

"I'll get there about one so we can discuss strategy," I say.

"And I have an idea that will make it look like I really do want to work for him, without having to give away any secrets about Sure Things, Inc.," Manny tells me. "See ya."

I hang up. Normally, I probably would not get out of bed for another hour or two on a Saturday, but I am wide awake. Today we finally get to learn who NAT DEFINITE is. I get to test my Invisibility Spray "in the field," as

Manny calls it, and maybe we can put this whole Definite Devices mystery behind us.

Downstairs I find Mom and Dad drinking hot chocolate.

"Well, look who's up early on a Saturday," says Dad. "What's the occasion?"

It's at that moment I realize I have not kept Mom and Dad up to speed on all the Definite Devices stuff. Emily, of course, knows all about it, but she's still sleeping.

"I have to meet Manny at the office a little later," I say. "We have to clean up some business from last week."

Don't get me wrong. I don't like keeping stuff from my parents, and technically what I told them is true. It's just too complicated a situation. And one that I really don't understand yet. So I'd rather wait until I have something definite to tell them. And I do mean "Definite!"

"Did someone call a family meeting without telling me?" says Emily, who walks slowly down the stairs, rubbing her eyes.

"Nope," I say, grabbing a box of cereal from the pantry.

"I made some TURKEY, KALE, AND BOLOGNA MUFFINS," Dad says proudly. "They're right there on the counter."

"Thanks," I say, putting away the cereal, not wanting to hurt Dad's feelings.

"Oh," says Emily, taking a muffin with one hand and the salt shaker full of Gross-to-Good Powder in the other. "Anything *definite* going on, Billy?"

"As a matter of fact, yes," I say, shaking some of the powder onto my muffin. "Nat Definite finally reached out to us. We're going to meet him today."

"Who's Nat Definite?" asks Mom.

See? Complicated.

"That is what I'm going to find out today," I say.

A little while later, with Philo trotting beside me, I hop on my bike and take off, looking forward to finally getting some answers.

I arrive at the office with plenty of time

to get invisible before Nat arrives. Manny is already here, hard at work on his laptop.

"Check this out, Billy," Manny says.

I lean over his shoulder and stare at a series of financial spreadsheets.

"I've spent the morning creating a fake set of financial reports for Sure Things, Inc.," he explains, pointing at columns of sales figures, marketing info, and new product ideas, all of which are made up. "This way Nat can see what I do, but we won't be giving any secrets away to a competitor."

"RECHARGEABLE GUM?" I ask, spotting one of the fake inventions that Sure Things, Inc. is supposedly working on.

"You know, a piece of gum that you could charge up again with flavor," Manny explains.

"But why wouldn't you just eat another piece of gum?" I ask. "Wouldn't that just be so much easier?"

"Hey, I was in a hurry," Many says, smiling.

That's Manny, putting the finishing touches onto his spreadsheet. Finally, everything is ready. At about a quarter to two I pull out the prototype can of Invisibility Spray.

"Okay, here goes," I say. Then I spray myself head to toe. A few seconds later I VANISH.

"Can you see me?" I ask.

"No," says Manny. "But I can sure smell you."

"Smell me?"

"Well, not *you*, but the bacon you used in the formula," Manny explains.

I raise my invisible hand to my nose and sniff. Manny is right. I can clearly smell bacon. I can see how that might be a drawback for people hoping to remain undetectable while they are invisible. I'll have to work that out later, and hope that for now, Nat Definite doesn't have a great sense of smell.

Philo certainly does, though.

Even thought he can't see me, Philo trots right over and licks my leg. All dogs have an incredible sense of smell. And Philo *loves* bacon. As a matter of fact, he looks a little disappointed that I only smell like bacon and that I don't actually taste like bacon.

Yeah, that is going to need some work.

Philo suddenly stops licking my bacon-scented leg. He turns around and starts barking and growling.

"RUFFF! RUFFF! GRRRRRRR!!"

"What is it, boy?" I ask. "You've been doing this all week, acting like you see something, but there is never anything there? What is going on with you?"

"RUFF! GRRR!"

Philo's growls and barks get louder.

"All right, I'll look over into that corner

that you've been barking at all week," I say. "But there's not going to be anything there."

I turn and look in the direction in which Philo has been barking.

Only there is something there.

Or rather, *someone*.

Chapter Ten

Nat Definite

"WHO ARE YOU?" I DEMAND, STARING RIGHT AT THE someone. She is tall, with bright red hair cut short around her face. She appears to be about my age. "And how did you get in here without me seeing you?"

"Um, I'm your partner, Manny," says Manny, who has his back to me and the girl. "And I was here when you got here. Has that bacon scent done something weird to your brain, too?"

"No, Manny, I'm not talking to you, I'm talking to *her*," I say, pointing right at the girl.

Manny spins around in his chair and looks

right in the direction where the girl is standing.

"Talking to who?" Manny asks. "You and I are the only ones here, other than Philo, of course."

"No, Manny," I say, and that's when it hits me. Manny can't see the girl because she is invisible too! I *can* see her because I'm also invisible.

Philo stares at the girl and snarls in her direction.

"OH, FISH STICKS!'" moans the girl. She sighs, her shoulders slumping. "Yes, Billy, you're right. I'm invisible, and now that you are, you can see me."

"That explains everything," I say. "Well, not everything. Like, who are you and what are you doing here?!"

"My name is NATALIA DEFINITE," says the girl. "But most people just call me Nat."

"Wait, *you're* Nat Definite?!" I exclaim, stunned not only by the fact that she is invisible and standing in our corner, but that this "guy" we were expecting to meet is actually a girl! "Well, that explains a lot. And I am pretty impressed that you invented an invisibility formula. So yours is a cream, huh?"

"Yup, and it doesn't smell like bacon," Nat says, waving her hands in front of her nose. "Yuck. I happen to be a vegetarian."

I pick up my prototype can of Invisibility Spray and I notice Nat picking up a white jar with a label that says "Invisibility Cream." She does make an interesting point.

And then a series of revelations come clear in my head, all at once.

"You're the one Philo's been growling at all week," I say, finally putting two and two together. "You've been here, invisible, spying on our office all week, haven't you? You're the one who's been moving stuff, and you're the one who got that quesadilla for Manny!"

Nat looks down at her feet.

"Yeah, I did bring Manny that quesadilla, and I didn't like looking at that picture of you and Manny together looking so happy, so I put it in the closet," she admits. "And yes, your dumb dog could smell me when I was invisible, even though I don't smell like bacon."

"But WHY?" I ask. "And why are you trying to steal my CFO away from me?"

"Um, excuse me," Manny says. "But I'd like to be part of this conversation, since it involves me. And I'd like to see who I'm talking to."

"Oh, right," I say. "Sorry, Manny." I turn to Nat.

"How long does your Invisibility Cream last?" I ask.

"It's timed to last for thirty minutes for

each dab you use," Nat says. "How about your spray?"

"Actually, I'm not sure how long it would last if I just left it, which is why I also invented Anti-Invisibility Spray," I explain. "That allows me to become visible again any time I want."

"Um, I think *now* would be a great time," says Manny.

"Oh, sorry!"

I spray myself with Anti-Invisibility Spray.

"Can I spray you, too?" I ask Nat. "I mean now that we both know you're here, there's really no point in you staying invisible."

"Sure," she says.

I spray Nat, and she too reappears.

"Hi, Manny," she says, smiling sheepishly, giving him a small wave of her hand.

"Hello, Natalia," says Manny.

"Call me Nat, please," she says. "Only my mother still calls me Natalia, and only when she's upset with me."

"Okay, Nat Definite, so what do we do

now?" Manny asks, getting up from his desk and joining us.

I notice that the bacon smell that had been reeking from me is gone. Maybe the Anti-Invisibility spray removed the smell? I'll have to look into that, but right now we've got more urgent business. And I do mean BUSINESS!

"You're here," Manny continues. "It's obvious that you've been spying on us, that you've been competing with Sure Things, Inc., that you made Kathy Jenkins fake an article, and that you're trying to get me to join your company. But why? And what do you really want?"

Nat's shoulders slump a bit. She obviously did not expect to get caught. And now the time has come to tell the truth.

"Well, Manny," Nat says, "I *have* been trying to steal you away from Sure Things, Inc. And I *am* also an inventor who has come up with a way to make people invisible."

"But why?" I ask, watching Philo retreat to his doggy bed now that I no longer smell of bacon. "Why are you trying to steal Manny?"

"A couple of reasons," Nat says. Then, quieter, "First, I think Manny is pretty cute."

WHAT?! I can't believe she's doing all this because she has a crush on Manny! I mean, it's not that I'm surprised that a girl has a crush on Manny, but what kind of business plan is that? Print lies, steal a business partner, all because you think he's cute?

I look over at Manny. His expression has not changed even one little bit. Like me, he's waiting, hoping there are better reasons for all Nat has done.

She goes on:

"But that's not all. According to what I've heard, Manny is the whole reason that Sure Things, Inc. is successful. So I want him to be on *my* team! I'm a better inventor than you, Billy. Together, Manny and I can be unstoppable."

I don't think I've ever met anyone quite like her. She's so . . . so . . . *direct*. I'm not sure if I like her—not that it really matters. Anyway, she doesn't wait for a reaction from me. She goes on.

"I can do my inventing when I'm awake. I don't need to sleep-invent. I'm *better*," she says.

What's wrong with sleep-inventing? I'm beginning to think that maybe I *don't* like Nat after all.

Again, she continues.

"My Invisibility Cream is better than your spray. It's made with TOP SECRET INGRE-DIENTS. I came up with it all by myself before I'd even heard of Manny Reyes. It works faster, it only requires a little dab on your hand for your whole body, and it doesn't smell like breakfast."

I really don't know what to think. No one has ever talked to me like this before. But the thing is . . . she's not wrong.

I look over at Manny, then back at Nat. Now I'm starting to feel nervous. Maybe Manny *would* be more successful at Definite Devices. Maybe he would have more fun crunching numbers with a better inventor. Maybe he wouldn't have to worry about the Next Big Thing anymore because the other inventor would already have it underway—without having to sleep-invent.

I have to say something. Manny was my best friend long before he was my business partner. I will always want what's best for Manny, no matter what it means for me.

"Manny," I say, hardly believing the words as they come out of my mouth. "If you think Definite Devices would be a better place for you, then you should GO BE THEIR CFO."

Chapter Eleven

a Definite Deal

MANNY, WHOSE EXPRESSION HASN'T CHANGED SINCE Nat appeared, shakes his head.

"I appreciate you looking out for me, Billy," he says.

Then he turns to Nat.

"But Nat, if you want to know why Sure Things, Inc. is so successful, here's the secret," Manny says. "It's not because I'm good with numbers or because Billy is good at inventing."

Nat's eyes open wide. She tilts her head a little and stares at Manny. "So what is it?" she finally says.

"It's because we're BEST FRIENDS," Manny explains. "Best friends who work together to create something we both love. Everything we do comes out of our friendship."

Nat's face scrunches up a bit. She looks confused.

Manny goes on. I know way better than to interrupt him when he is on a roll like this one, so I'm silent.

"Nat, you're obviously a really good inventor. But no matter what I know or what I'm able to do, I am not the right CFO for you and your company. The right CFO for you is someone you're close to. Someone you enjoy spending time with and working with day after day after day."

"Like me," says a small, high-pitched voice from across the room.

I spin around and look over at the spot where the voice came from. I see no one. There's another invisible person in this office?! This is just too much.

"Where are you?" I ask.

"Right here," replies the voice, now obviously just a few feet away from where I'm standing. It would be creepy if it wasn't so cool that being invisible can be a reality now.

I realize that I am still holding the can of Anti-Invisibility Spray in my hand. I lift it and spray in the direction of the voice. A few seconds later a short girl with black hair appears. She also looks to be about the same age as us.

"Who are you?" I ask. "And where were you hiding? I didn't see you when I was invisible."

"I was over there, behind the desk," says the girl, pointing back at the spot where her voice had originally come from. "Nat brought me along for support. I'm JADA PARIKH, Nat's best friend."

Manny and I shake Jada's hand.

"Nice to meet you," I say. "I think."

"We really didn't mean to do anything bad," Jada says. "It's just that, well, Nat really likes Manny and wants Definite Devices to be a successful business."

I'm not really sure what to say. After all

the wondering and worrying about Definite Devices and who Nat Definite is, now that we've finally met her and Jada, it's clear they're not bad people. Nat might be a little sneaky, but not bad. She only wants for her company what I want for Sure Things, Inc.— success and Manny.

As usual, Manny comes up with the perfect thing to say.

"I have an idea that might make everyone happy, and could benefit both of our companies," he begins. Nat and Jada stare at Manny, hanging on his every word.

"Of course, Billy, this has to be okay with you," Manny goes on. "But here's my idea. We come out with a joint product produced by Sure Things, Inc. and Definite Devices. We can call it a DEFINITELY SURE PRODUCT."

I'm not 100 percent sure I like this idea, but I am impressed, as always, that Manny has already come up with a name for this joint product, and that he probably has half of the marketing plan ready in his head.

Manny continues. "What if we put Nat's odorless Invisibility Cream into a spray bottle?" he says. "And we'll sell it in a kit with Billy's Anti-Invisibility Spray. This would combine both of our inventions perfectly."

"I like this," I say. "What about the business side?"

"We'll release the product together and share all of the profits fifty-fifty," Manny replies.

"Makes sense," I say. Pretty simple. But Manny is not done yet.

"In addition, I'd be happy to mentor Jada on how to be the best CFO she can be—for Definite Devices, that is. That way, Nat, you will be working closely with your best friend, just like Billy and I do."

Jada smiles, her face beaming.

"But the Definitely Sure product will just be a ONE-TIME THING," Manny says. "After this product, we'll go back to being competitors, and a little competition never hurt anyone. At that point, may the best company win! Sound good?"

It sure does. The more Manny talks, the more my doubts disappear. Turning lemons into lemonade: Reason #714 why I'm glad that Manny is my best friend.

"That's amazing!" says Jada. "What you just did there, Manny. That is so cool. And I can't thank you enough for offering to mentor me as a CFO."

Nat has remained quiet throughout Manny's whole speech. We all turn and look at her now. She is not smiling. In fact, she looks kinda grumpy. It's the same expression Emily usually has when she isn't being ULTRA SUPER NICE EMILY.

"What do you think, Nat?" I ask. "Does this sound okay? Do we have a deal?"

"I think it's a good idea, I guess," Nat says. "It does sound like a win-win situation for all of us."

She still doesn't sound happy.

"I just wish I got to spend more time with you, Manny," Nat admits.

I turn toward Manny. He is BLUSHING.

I have to admit, in all the time we've been friends, I don't think I've ever seen him look this uncomfortable.

I laugh. Jada laughs. Even Manny manages a smile. Only Nat is not laughing. Having revealed that she really likes Manny, she seems anxious to turn the conversation back to business.

"I agree. Let's do this joint product," she says finally. "I'll also make sure that Definite Devices sponsors a new article for Kathy Jenkins to write, revealing the truth about your successful partnership."

Finally, Manny will get recognized for what he does at Sure Things, Inc. without me looking like a bad guy. I guess I'd better prepare myself for Samantha Jenkins to start following me around the halls at school again.

"You guys are too good of a team to get such bad press like that," Nat continues. "I'm sorry I caused that to happen."

"Here, take a look at this," says Manny. He snatches a piece of paper from the printer and hands it to Nat. "It's just a simple one-page agreement for our two companies to work together to release the Definitely Sure Invisibility and Anti-Invisibility Sprays as a ONE-TIME PARTNERSHIP."

That's Manny. In the time it took Nat to apologize, he has already drafted an agreement.

"Looks good to me," says Nat.

"Maybe you should let your new CFO take a look at it," I suggest, smiling.

Nat hands the paper to Jada. She glances at it quickly.

"Well, you left out a period on this sentence, and these two columns of numbers don't exactly line up, but otherwise it's in pretty good shape," Jada says.

Manny laughs out loud. "Nat, I think you've got yourself a TOP-NOTCH CFO!"

Manny and Jada both sign the agreement, then Nat and I get to work combining our two formulas.

As it turns out, our two products are more similar than I originally thought. It only takes about an hour before the new, improved, non-stinky Invisibility Spray is ready.

"Time for a test," I say.

I'm about to spray some of the new formula on myself, when Philo hops out of his bed and decides that this is the perfect moment to jump up on me. Which he does, just as I spray.

The spray hits Philo instead of me. He instantly turns invisible.

"Oh, Philo!" I say. Normally, I would never, ever test a product on myself or Philo, but Sure products are something special. Just remember, don't try this at home! "Let me grab the Anti-Invisibility Spray."

But before I can reach it, Philo snatches the can in his mouth and runs across the office. Of course, all we see is a can ZIPPING through the air by itself.

"Come on, Philo, bring that back," I say. But he is obviously having too much fun to stop.

"I have an idea," says Nat.

She walks over to my workbench and grabs

a piece of bacon left over from my formula.

"Here, Philo," she says, waving the bacon back and forth down near the floor.

The can of Anti-Invisibility Spray comes zooming toward Nat and stops right at her feet.

"URRRR . . ."

I know that sound. That's Philo trying to figure out how he can eat the bacon without letting go of the can. It doesn't take him long to realize that he can't do both.

Can . . . bacon . . . can . . . bacon . . . no contest.

The can drops to the floor and Philo hungrily attacks his bacon. I pick up the can and spray it in the direction of the quickly disappearing piece of bacon. Philo reappears, licking his lips.

"Quick thinking, there, Nat," I tell her.

"Well, at least your bacon is good for something," she says. "Now, excuse me, I have to go wash my hands."

A short while later Philo and I head for home. I am so relieved that this all worked out. Mostly

I am relieved that my partnership with Manny is as solid as ever. And I'm excited about the upcoming release of the INVISIBILITY KIT (consisting of both sprays). Not to mention the success of the hovercraft toy—which just got a feature in *Toys, Toys, Toys* magazine!

I arrive at home to see Dad carrying one of his paintings. A rented van sits in the driveway with its back doors open.

"What's going on?" I ask, hopping off my bike.

"Just loading my paintings into the van to bring them to the art gallery," says Dad. He slips a painting of Philo's back foot into the van right next to a painting of a curried salmon muffin he made last week.

Emily comes bursting from the house.

"Here, Dad, let me help you with that," she says.

"All done, Em," says Dad. "That was the last one. Looks like you still have one more nice big thing you have to do for me before you can be ungrounded."

Emily smiles. "All right," she says. "I'm ready whenever you are."

Well, it looks like I'm going to have Ultra Super Nice Emily around for a little while longer. Which is a good thing to look forward to, at least . . . because I have a feeling Nat and Jada aren't done trying to steal Manny away from Sure Things, Inc.

My name is Billy Sure. Right now I'm sitting at my workbench at the World Headquarters of Sure Things, Inc. Across the room—which used to be the Reyes family garage—sits my best friend and business partner, Manny Reyes. Manny and I make up Sure Things, Inc., the world's only inventing company run by seventh graders—or so we thought.

We recently discovered that a company named Definite Devices also exists, and it is also run by two seventh graders—Nat Definite and Jada Parikh. And not only do they exist, but they were working on an invisibility invention at the same time Manny and I were at Sure Things, Inc.!

As you can imagine, that was kind of a problem. But Manny, being the genius chief financial officer he is, worked out a deal. We all agreed to release a joint invisibility invention produced by both Sure Things, Inc. and Definite Devices—the Definitely Sure Invisibility (and Anti-Invisibility) Sprays. We joined forces on this one project only.

Before our two companies agreed to work together, Nat did her best to try to steal Manny away from me—and from Sure Things, Inc! She wanted him to work with her over at Definite Devices, because . . . well, the obvious answer is that Manny is a brilliant CFO, business-person, marketing genius, computer whiz . . . but it's more than that.

Nat has a crush on Manny!

"That is the most beautiful spreadsheet I've ever seen, Manny," Nat says, her face glowing. (Oh yeah. Because we're technically partners and all, she's sitting at the World Headquarters now too.)

Jada, who Manny agreed to train as the CFO for Definite Devices, scrunches up her face.

"How can a spreadsheet be beautiful, Nat?" she asks. "It's just a series of numbers and pro-jections and—"

"Anything Manny does is beautiful," says Nat.

See what I mean?

"So, Jada," Manny begins, doing his best to

ignore Nat. "As you can see, we've placed the sprays in a few high-end specialty stores."

"To generate early buzz on social media," Jada adds.

"Exactly," Manny replies. "So by the time we release it to the major chains—"

"—people will be waiting in line to buy it," Jada finishes.

Jada's really smart. Like . . . Manny-smart.

Just then, a noise comes from Manny's phone.

Ping!

"Looks like we have another incident of someone using the Definitely Sure Invisibility Spray to cut a line," Manny says, frowning. "Last week someone used it at a movie theater. Now in a theme park."

"That's not good," I say. Then I get an idea. "Maybe the next batch of sprays can make kids who try to cut lines grow really big noses! Temporarily, of course."

"Great idea, *partner*," Manny says. "Maybe even a nose like an elephant trunk—that could make using the rides really hard!"

I might be imagining it, but I think he emphasized the word "partner" so that Nat and Jada would notice.

"All right, that's enough work for today," Manny adds with a smile.

I think what Manny really means is, You should go home now, Nat.

Nat frowns. But she can't complain, because she has been here for hours. She and Jada pack up and leave.

I'm just about to do my best Nat imitation, ("Manny, you are so, so funny!") when Briiiiing! Briiiing! My phone rings. Who could be calling now?

I pick up the phone, hoping the call has nothing to do with Definite Devices. Don't get me wrong—I'm happy there are other kids out there who are working on their dream. I've just kind of had enough of them for today.

"Hi, Billy?" comes a voice through the phone.

Hmm. It definitely doesn't sound like Nat

or Jada from Definite Devices! Who *is* this?

"Is this a good time to talk?" she asks, pronouncing every syllable clearly in a British accent. "It's Gemma Weston."

Gemma . . . *Weston?!*

She's only the most famous movie star in the whole world!

"Uh, hey, Gemma, how are you doing?" I say, thinking instantly that I sound like a major dork. I just so happen to be speaking to one of the world's biggest celebrities, and here I am, saying things like "uh, hey"!

"I'm well, thank you," Gemma replies. "I still think about the fun we had filming *Alien Zombie Attack!*"

Okay, explanation. Not too long ago, Manny, Emily, and I were extras in Gemma's film *Alien Zombie Attack!* as part of an agreement to let Sure Things, Inc.'s hovercraft invention be used in the film. While there, Emily and Gemma became close friends. And I hadn't realized it, but I'm now on a first name basis with Gemma Weston too!

"That was pretty fun, Gemma," I say. "I had a really good time making that movie. So, what's up?"

"If you remember, I told you that I'd love to work with Sure Things, Inc. again," Gemma says excitedly. "And the chance to work together has just come up! I've been asked to host a new TV show called *Sing Out and Shout*. It's airing live this weekend. It's a singing competition show."

"A singing competition show," I repeat. "Is it okay if I put you on speakerphone, Gemma? I'm at the Sure Things, Inc. office now and I'd love to have Manny listen in."

"Absolutely!" Gemma says.

Click. Her voice fills the open air.

"Hello, Manny! I was just telling Billy about a singing competition TV show I'm hosting. We are looking for celebrity contestants and celebrity judges, and I thought that you two might be interested," Gemma explains.

Celebrity judges?!

Did the mega movie star Gemma Weston

just call me a celebrity? I mean, tons of kids know my name because of my inventions and all that—but enough to be called a celebrity by an *actual* celebrity . . . that's a whole other level of cool!

"So, what do you think?" Gemma asks. "Can I count on you two to help me out this weekend?"

Manny and I exchange looks. The weekend is only a few days away. I'm ready to pipe up and scream YES!, but Manny looks a little concerned.

"Can you give us a second, Gemma?" I ask. I put the call on mute.

"What's the matter?" I ask Manny. "We always have a good time when we go on TV."

"Billy, I don't love being in the spotlight," Manny says. "Every time we've been on TV before, it's you who's been interviewed. I only agreed to *Alien Zombie Attack!* because we were dressed as zombies. And for our Next Big Thing show, I was promoting Sure Things, Inc. But for me personally to be on TV—I just don't know. . . ."

Huh. I never realized that Manny has a little bit of stage fright.

"But that's the beautiful thing about this show," I explain. "We won't be in the spotlight. The celebrity singers will be. And so this becomes awesome publicity for Sure Things, Inc., just as we are pushing the Really Great Hovercraft Toy and the Invisibility Kit. And all this, Manny, will be hosted by a big movie star!"

Okay, I guess that was all really Manny of me to say. Manny is usually the one to push publicity on me, but I think this makes sense. Also I really want to work with Gemma Weston again. I wouldn't admit this to anyone, but I might have a teeny-tiny crush on Gemma Weston, although it's nowhere near as big as the crush Nat has on Manny.

Manny thinks for a moment, then smiles. I can see him warming to this idea.

"Well, when you put it that way . . . ," he says. "All that publicity. Yeah, let's do it. After all, what can happen?"

"Score!" I shout. "I'll unmute us now."

I quickly hit a button on my phone and the call goes live again.

"Well, that was fast," Gemma says.

"Yeah, it didn't take long for us to figure out that this is a great idea. Manny and I would love to be on *Sing Out and Shout*. Sign us up!"

"That's fantastic, Team Sure Things, Inc.," she says. "I just know you two are going to have a great time. And also, one request?" she asks. "Please invite Emily to the show on my behalf. I really miss her. And it's strange—lately it seems that her phone is always off. That's not like Em at all."

I really wasn't kidding when I said Emily and Gemma are BFFs.

She's right, of course. Emily's phone *has* been off. That's because she's been grounded. Remember when I said we were extras on Gemma's film? Well, we weren't supposed to be—a few weeks ago, Emily stole my hovercraft invention and crash-landed at the studio. Dad let us be in the movie, but after Emily's little bout of—you know—stealing my hovercraft—he grounded her "for life." I don't think he's *too* serious about the "for life" sentence, though, because later he said that if she is as nice as she can possibly be and does one nice big thing for everyone in the family, she can be off her punishment.

But until then, no phone. I'm not going to tell Gemma that. Despite the fact that Emily and I don't always get along— did I mention that she's my big sister?—I don't need to embarrass her.

"I'll definitely relay the message, Gemma," I say.

"Great. Thanks. I'll send you the schedule for the show soon. See ya, Billy and Manny!"

"Bye, Gemma," Manny and I say in unison.

Bye, Gemma. How cool is that!

I stand near the door with a huge smile on my face. That's when I notice something—it's really late! I hardly noticed the time passing with all of the guests today at the office.

"Uh, I should go home now," I say, feeling a

little foolish, standing there in a daze because I just got off the phone with Gemma Weston. "See ya tomorrow, Manny. Come on, Philo!"

My dog, Philo, who always comes with me to the Sure Things, Inc. office, follows me out the door. I hop onto my bike and head for home.

At home I run into Emily in the upstairs hallway. Or at least, I *think* I run into Emily. It could also be a flamingo. Or a Pekingese dog. Or an ostrich. But since none of those options really make sense, I decide it's Emily wearing a really strange-looking hat. The hat has three flowers growing out the front and a statue of a bird with its wings spread open on the back.

This? This has got to be Emily's next "thing." My sister has always had a "thing," like speaking with a British accent, or wearing glasses with no lenses, or apparently wearing a hat that makes her look like a flamingo-Pekingese-ostrich hybrid. Thankfully, Emily's things are gone as quickly as they come. And for her sake, I'm hoping this one goes fast.

"You're never going to believe who called me today," I begin, doing my best not to laugh.

"Dad?" Emily replies. "Saying I'm finally ungrounded and can have my phone back?"

"Sorry, no," I say. "It was Gemma Weston!"

Emily's expression immediately changes. "She called you? Why did she call you?"

"She asked Manny and me to be on her new TV show. Isn't that cool?"

Emily's eyes flash. Emily is Sure Things, Inc.'s Very Official Hollywood Coordinator, so technically, booking a TV show falls into her realm of business at Sure Things, Inc. But I think she's so upset about her phone—or maybe she's so tired from wearing that heavy hat all day—that she doesn't say anything.

I continue.

"And Gemma invited you to come to the TV show as her special guest, too," I say. "But it airs this weekend . . ."

"No! That does it!" Emily screeches. "I have got to get out of this grounded-for-life punishment by then!"

She storms into her room and slams the door shut.

You're welcome, I think.

Did you LOVE reading this book?

Visit the Whyville...

IN THE MIDDLE BOOK HIVE

Where you can:

- Discover great books!
- Meet new friends!
- Read exclusive sneak peeks and more!

Log on to visit now!
bookhive.whyville.net

DATE	ISSUED TO
1951	Matt Vezza
1977	Jada Reese
1696	Luis Ramirez

TIME MACHINES MAY BE HARD TO INVENT, BUT TIME TRAVEL STORIES AREN'T! GO BACK IN TIME ON HILARIOUS ADVENTURES WITH THE STUDENTS OF SANDS MIDDLE SCHOOL IN